GROLIER
B O O K S

Deep in the jungle, surrounded by mountains and rivers, stood the palace of young Emperor Kuzco. He was very rich and always got what he wanted.

Kuzco was the all-powerful ruler of everything and everyone. But in his perfect world, nothing was ever good enough for him. One day several beautiful young maidens were presented to him as possible brides. The emperor looked at the maidens and rudely insulted each one.

The only time Kuzco seemed satisfied was when he had dozens of servants waiting on him and giving him compliments.

When Emperor
Kuzco wasn't sitting
on his throne shouting
orders, his advisor,
Yzma, was there
instead. She wanted
to take over the royal
power. As always,
Yzma's handsome
assistant, Kronk, was
right beside her.

One day,
Kuzco became
annoyed when he
caught Yzma on
his throne. So he
fired her.

"You're being let
go," he told her
casually.

Yzma was
shocked . . . and
furious!

On the same
day, a peasant
named Pacha
arrived at the
palace. Kuzco had
ordered Pacha to
come from his
distant home to
answer just one
question.

Showing the peasant a model of his hilltop village, Kuzco asked Pacha where the sun shone best.

After Pacha answered politely, the emperor smiled. "I just needed an insider's opinion before I okayed the spot for my pool." Then he slammed a model of his new summer home on top of the village.

Pacha was shocked! Kuzco was going to destroy his village. "But where will we live?" he protested.

Unfortunately, Kuzco didn't care.

Meanwhile, hidden away in her laboratory beneath the palace, Yzma was plotting to get rid of Kuzco. She and Kronk found a vial containing a deadly poison.

Yzma invited Kuzco to dinner that evening. Once Kuzco arrived, Kronk served him a drink containing the poison.

But the bumbling Kronk had put the wrong potion
in the emperor's drink. It wasn't a poison at all. But it
did turn Kuzco into a long-eared llama!

Yzma stared at the llama in shock. "Hit him on the
head," she whispered to Kronk. Then she told Kronk
to stuff the llama in a sack and get rid of him.

Kronk lugged the sack to a large waterfall
and threw it in. Suddenly he felt guilty. Quickly
grabbing the sack out of the water, he ran through
town wondering what to do. He raced down some
stairs, tripped over a cat, and dropped the sack. The
sack with Kuzco inside landed on the back of Pacha's
cart. Before Kronk could stop him, Pacha had left.

When Pacha arrived home, he was surprised to discover the unconscious llama in his cart.

"Where did you come from, little guy?" he asked, stroking Kuzco's mane.

Kuzco woke up—and spoke! "No touchy!" he yelled.

"Aah! Demon llama!" Pacha cried, staring at Kuzco.

"Where?" Kuzco shrieked. Then he saw his reflection in some water and realized *he* was the llama!

"Okay, demon llama, just take it easy. I mean you no harm," Pacha said gently.

"What are you talking about?" Kuzco snapped. "Oh, wait! I know you. You're that whiny peasant!"

"Emperor Kuzco?" Pacha gasped, surprised.

But Kuzco thought Pacha was trying to trick him. "I remember telling you that I was building my pool where your house was, and then you got mad at me —oh!—and then you turned me into a llama! And then you kidnapped me!" Kuzco cried.

"No, I did not!" Pacha replied angrily.

Kuzco wanted to return to his palace. He thought
Yzma could change him back into a human. He
didn't suspect Yzma of trying to kill him in the first
place! Kuzco demanded that Pacha take him home.

"Only if you build your summer house somewhere
else," Pacha replied.

Kuzco refused. He trotted off—alone—towards
the palace, despite Pacha's warning about the dangers
of the jungle.

It wasn't long before Kuzco realized the jungle was scarier than he had thought.

"AAH!" he shrieked as a little squirrel appeared from the bushes, surprising him. The squirrel offered Kuzco an acorn. "Get lost, Bucky!" the emperor rudely replied.

At that moment, Kuzco fell down a hill and landed in the middle of a pack of hungry jaguars. Kuzco ran, but he ended up trapped at the edge of a steep cliff.

Luckily, Pacha had been worried about
Kuzco, so he had secretly followed him. With
an "Aaaaahhhh!" Pacha swung down on a
vine and snatched Kuzco from the jaguars!

But the rescue didn't go quite as planned.
The pair ended up lashed to a branch, and it was
about to break! With a scream, they dropped into
the river far below. Kuzco was *not* pleased.

They were carried, swirling and dipping, through the water until Pacha finally managed to drag Kuzco out. And when Kuzco didn't wake up, Pacha almost had to revive him with the "kiss of life." *Yuck!* Luckily, Kuzco woke up just in time and no "kiss" was needed.

Back at the palace, Yzma was furious. Kronk
had just told her that Kuzco wasn't really dead.
"You and I are going out to find him!" she
shouted. "If he talks, we're through!"

Out in the jungle, Kuzco and Pacha were shivering by a small fire. When Pacha gave the freezing llama his poncho to keep warm, Kuzco was surprised. He wondered about Pacha's kindness. But that didn't stop him from lying to the peasant. Kuzco told Pacha that he'd decided not to destroy Pacha's village.

The two shook hands on it. Believing Kuzco, Pacha agreed to take him to the palace.

The next day, as they were in sight of the palace, Pacha fell through a hole in a bridge. Dangling above a river, he shouted to Kuzco, "Quick, help me up!"

"No," Kuzco replied, "I don't think I will." Kuzco didn't care about Pacha. He had never intended to keep his promise to spare Pacha's village.

"So it was all a lie?" Pacha asked.

"Well, yeah," Kuzco replied.

Suddenly the bridge gave way beneath Kuzco. "AAH!" he yelled as he dangled over the river with Pacha. The pair had to work together to save their lives. But when they reached the top, the edge of the cliff gave way! Pacha started to fall, but Kuzco pulled him to safety. "You just saved my life," Pacha told Kuzco. "There is some good in you after all."

After their adventures, Pacha and Kuzco were starving. They went to a jungle restaurant—but llamas weren't allowed inside. So Pacha disguised Kuzco as his bride.

Kuzco decided the food wasn't up to his standards. He went to scold the cook in the kitchen. Just then, Yzma and Kronk came into the restaurant. Pacha overheard them plotting to kill the emperor!

Thinking quickly, Pacha told the waitress that it was Yzma's birthday. As the waiter and waitress sang and congratulated Yzma, Pacha sneaked the unsuspecting Kuzco outside.

Then Pacha described the strange couple in the restaurant to the emperor.

"That's Yzma and Kronk!" Kuzco exclaimed. "I'm saved."

"They're trying to kill you," Pacha argued. But Kuzco didn't believe him and hurried back to find Yzma. When he overheard Yzma and Kronk talking, he realized that the peasant was right. But by then Pacha had gone.

Unfortunately, Kronk had seen Pacha in the restaurant and finally remembered him. Pacha was the peasant who had driven away with the llama in his cart.

"If we find his village," Kronk thought out loud, "we find him. And if we find him, we find Kuzco!"

Soon they were in Pacha's village, sitting in his house and pretending to be relatives.

"Why, I'm his third cousin's brother's wife's step-niece's great-aunt. Twice removed," Yzma lied to Pacha's wife, Chicha.

Meanwhile, Pacha and Kuzco had found each other and made up. As they returned to Pacha's house for supplies, they saw Kronk and Yzma. Pacha signalled to his wife to meet him alone.

Then Pacha secretly asked Chicha to distract Yzma and Kronk. That way he and Kuzco could get a head start back to the palace.

So Pacha's clever wife and kids locked Yzma in a room . . . and when Yzma managed to break out, they had a surprise of honey and feathers waiting for her!

But Yzma wasn't
about to give up!

Soon she and Kronk were chasing
Pacha and Kuzco through the jungle.

It seemed nothing could stop her! But happily for Pacha and Kuzco, a bolt of lightning did!

Arriving at the palace at last, Pacha and Kuzco hurried to Yzma's laboratory. They began looking for a potion that would change the emperor back into a human. But the laboratory was full of potions! As the pair searched, Yzma and Kronk turned up.

"Finish them off!" Yzma ordered her assistant.

Kronk, however, was having second thoughts.

Yzma finally lost
patience and pulled a lever.
"I should have seen that
coming," Kronk said as he
fell down a deep shaft.

Then Yzma called in her guards to get rid of Pacha and Kuzco. The pair was in real trouble now. They began tossing vials of potions at the guards.

POOF! POOF! POOF! POOF! POOF!

The guards changed into a warthog, a lizard, a cow, an ostrich, and an octopus! But Kuzco and Pacha still weren't safe.

"Get them!" Yzma yelled at the animal guards.

The guards chased the pair outside to the front of
the palace. Pacha and Kuzco managed to climb onto
a ledge thousands of feet above the ground. They had
two vials left. But Yzma knocked the vials away. As
she and Kuzco sprang for them, they butted heads.

Yzma fell on top of one of the vials. *POOF!* She
was changed into a hissing, spitting kitten.

"I'll take that," Kuzco said, reaching for the last vial.

Just then Yzma the cat jumped onto his head. When Pacha tried to pull her off the llama, the peasant stumbled and fell off the ledge.

Pacha dangled far above the ground, barely hanging on. "Drink the potion!" he yelled to Kuzco.

After a struggle with Yzma, the last vial was within Kuzco's reach—but Pacha needed his help. Instead of grabbing the potion, Kuzco grabbed his friend.

Pacha couldn't believe it. The emperor had saved him instead of drinking the potion. Kuzco had actually done his second unselfish act—and all for his friend, Pacha.

But now Yzma the cat had the potion! "I win!" she shouted. It seemed all hope of getting the potion was gone.

But then Kronk
opened a door, flattening
Yzma behind it. She
dropped the vial, which
Pacha caught and handed
to Kuzco. He drank it,
and the llama turned back
into the young emperor!

Soon Kuzco was
looking at the model of
his summer home again.
Only this time . . .

. . . the emperor was grateful to Pacha. The peasant had not only helped him regain his human form, but he had also taught him that kindness and friendship are the most valuable things in the world.

So when Kuzco built his new summer home, it was a modest hut on the hill next to Pacha's village.

Pacha and his family and friends were happy to celebrate this newfound happiness with Kuzco.

Kronk was happy, too. He became a scout leader to all the kids in Pacha's village. Yzma the cat stayed at the village, too. She even attended Kronk's scout meetings once in a while.